W9-CEV-735

WITHDRAWN FROM COLLECTION

Xander and the Rainbow-Barfing Unicorns is published by
Stone Arch Books
a Capstone imprint
1710 Roe Crest Drive
North Mankato, Minnesota 56003
www.mycapstone.com

Copyright © 2019 by Stone Arch Books.

All rights reserved. No part of this publication may be
reproduced in whole or in part, or stored in a retrieval
system, or transmitted in any form or by any means,
electronic, mechanical, photocopying, recording, or
otherwise, without written permission of the publisher.

Cataloging-in-Publication Data is available on the Library
of Congress website.
ISBN 978-1-4965-5712-4 (library binding)
ISBN 978-1-4965-5716-2 (paperback)
ISBN 978-1-4965-5728-5 (eBook PDF)

Summary: Xander is the only person on Earth who knows
about the Rainbow-Barfing Unicorns. Except, of course,
for a rich and crazy billionaire who will stop at nothing
to capture these zombielike, upchucking creatures and get
even richer and crazier!

Designer: Bob Lentz
Production Specialist: Kris Wilfahrt

Printed and bound in Canada. PA020

by Matthew K. Manning

Illustrated by Joey Ellis

REVENGE
OF THE
ONE TRICK
PONY

STONE ARCH BOOKS
a capstone imprint

The Rainbow-Barfing Unicorns
come from a faraway, magical
world called Pegasia. Not so long
ago, these stinky, zombielike,
upchucking creatures were
banished to Earth for being,
well . . . stinky, zombielike,
upchucking creatures. However,
Earth presents them with a new
danger: humans.

So, just who are the Rainbow-Barfing
Unicorns . . . ?

CRADIE

(CRAY-DEE)

BLEP

(BLEHP)

RONK

(RAWNK)

CHAPTER ONE

Mrs. DeVon stared into her morning coffee. As usual, she had no expression on her face. She looked neither sad nor happy. This was simply the state of things for her these days.

She had long stopped crying. Now, she felt nothing at all. Mrs. DeVon imagined she would never feel anything again.

She had been like that since Russ had gone missing. He was her baby boy. Mrs. DeVon had been an overprotective mom—she could admit that now.

Russ was on a very strict diet. He was never allowed to go to a sleepover at a friend's house or on a field trip with his fourth-grade class. Mrs. DeVon would pick him up every day, even if that meant waiting in a long line of cars filled with equally eager parents.

"The bus would be so much quicker," Russ would say. But Mrs. DeVon would not have it.

So Russ would usually pout a bit. Then he would head up to his room to write or draw in that favorite blue notebook of his.

But in the end, none of it had mattered. Despite her best efforts, Russ had gone missing over a month ago.

There was a large field outside the DeVons' house. Soybeans grew there, although the property belonged to the neighbors. The DeVon family had a small lot of land. Mr. DeVon worked at the welding plant in town, and land was cheap in that part of Ohio.

They could afford a little house, but not much more. Mrs. DeVon had loved that house. Now she didn't seem to care about anything at all.

That's the reason Mrs. DeVon wasn't paying attention when a little boy fell out of the sky and into the bean field.

Russ woke up with a face full of mud and a particularly jagged soybean stalk poking through his favorite light jacket. He stood up and blinked. He patted his jacket, as if to check for something. His stomach ached.

Then he noticed the pain in his index finger. He stuck it in his mouth. It had a pinprick on its end that stung just the tiniest bit.

Without the slightest emotion, Russ walked toward the back of his house. He didn't bother to jump across the backyard's stepping stones. He didn't swat at the low-hanging branches of his favorite willow tree. He didn't even bother to bend down and pet his cat, Jeffrey Paddypaws, when Jeff came brushing up against his leg. Russ simply walked in through the back door.

Mrs. DeVon lifted her coffee cup up to her lips. She stared at the rose-colored wallpaper below her kitchen cabinets. She didn't react at first when she heard the door open. She even didn't move until she heard the familiar squeak of Russ' sneakers.

When she finally looked over her shoulder, a shiver went down her entire body. She set her mug down a little too hard. A bit of the warm coffee splashed onto the counter. And then she leaped out of her seat and nearly tackled her boy.

Russ didn't try to move. He stood there and let his mother hug him. But after five minutes, enough was enough. He had things to do.

"Mom," he said.

"Oh my little Russ," she was saying. She had been saying that over and over during their hug. He had gotten the gist of it by now.

"Mom," he said again. Russ stood up straight, as straight as any nine-year-old boy could possibly get. "I need to get to my room."

Mrs. DeVon let go of her son, at least a little bit. She still held his shoulders in her hands, but she wasn't hugging him any longer. (Not technically.)

"Where have you been?" she said, tears still streaming down her face.

"We can talk about that later," said Russ. His voice was calm.

It almost made Mrs. DeVon feel like she was overreacting. Almost.

"What do you—?"

"Mom," Russ repeated. His voice was approaching something in the stern range. "I need to get up to my room. I have a story I need to write down."

Mrs. DeVon let her boy go. But she followed him to his room. And she sat there in the corner while her boy—her baby boy—wrote page after page in his favorite blue notebook.

CHAPTER TWO

Aunt Melinda only had two nieces, but it certainly didn't seem like it. Everyone Xander knew called her "Aunt." If she had it her way, Xander's entire sixth-grade class would be invited over for family movie night. As it was, only Xander's classmate Kelly and her little sister, Emily, were Aunt Melinda's true flesh and blood.

Melinda was a friendly sort. Xander assumed a person had to be if they ran an apple orchard. Orchards required happy customers to stay in business. Happy customers required happy employees to assist them in their apple-picking needs. And happy employees required a happy boss to keep them that way.

Xander had been working for the Montgomery Apple Orchard and Farm for over a month now. In that entire time, he had yet to see Aunt Melinda frown. But today, she was close to it.

As she weaved through the crowd of people toward the Henderson Landfill—the dump that neighbored her orchard—Aunt Melinda's smile bordered on an angry grimace. She still managed to greet every paying customer with a friendly "hello" said through a Southern drawl. If they had truly known her, the guests would have noticed that she didn't really mean it.

Aunt Melinda was in a hurry today, and it was all Xander's fault.

"Xander!" she called as she pulled open the gate door to the dump.

"RONK!" came the response.

It wasn't Xander speaking, of course. It was one of his famous Rainbow-Barfing Unicorns. It was the green one with the uneven eyes. His name was easy enough to remember. It was simply Ronk.

Aunt Melinda had never said as much, but Ronk creeped her out. She wasn't sure how Xander pulled off his magic tricks with these sickly-looking ponies. She figured it didn't matter. Nor did her feelings on the subject make much of a difference.

The audience absolutely loved the boy's little stage show. It was hard enough getting customers to an orchard neighboring a landfill. It was even harder to get them to stick around. Xander and his Rainbow-Barfing Unicorns had practically saved the Montgomery Apple Orchard and Farm from bankruptcy. Aunt Melinda owed Xander big time. That was the only reason she wasn't yelling at him at the moment.

She saw Ronk first, when he stepped out from behind a huge stack of mattresses.

"RONK!" he said again. It was the only thing he could say, Aunt Melinda knew. Of course it was. To her, he was just a pony wearing a fake unicorn horn. He couldn't truly say anything.

Aunt Melinda was right about a great many things. But the Rainbow-Barfing Unicorns were not on that list. Xander coated them in a good amount of stage makeup to hide the fact that the unicorns were actually zombies from another dimension. But he couldn't hide their horns. The audience thought it was all part of the show.

They, and Aunt Melinda, assumed that during the performance's big finale, Xander had worked out some sort of device that projected rainbows from his ponies' mouths. None of the guests at the Montgomery Orchard ever suspected that these weird, mythical creatures actually barfed real rainbows.

Ronk was all made up for the show already. Which was a good thing, because Xander was supposed to have drawn the opening curtain nearly five minutes ago.

The green unicorn was smiling at Aunt Melinda. The weird cracked and dry patches on his skin were covered up nicely by Xander's powder and makeup. He looked almost clean. The makeup didn't do anything about his smell, however.

Aunt Melinda got a big whiff of that particularly unfriendly aroma as she hurried past him. If human feet could spoil, that's exactly what Ronk smelled like.

"Xander!" Melinda called again. Behind her, Ronk ronked once more.

"Oh, hey," said Xander as Melinda rounded a corner past a broken-down refrigerator and a large, empty wooden crate. "What's up?"

Xander was currently fluffing Cradie in the face with a powder puff. The purple unicorn looked fairly presentable despite her strangely matted green mane.

Next to them was Blep, the third of the unicorn trio. His makeup had already been smoothed over his reddish hide. He still seemed a little rough around the edges, but it would have to do. Blep always looked rough around the edges.

"You're late!" Melinda said. And that was all she had come there to say. She turned dramatically. Her gray ponytail whipped the air, as if to gesture, "Follow me!"

Realizing Aunt Melinda was correct, Xander did what the ponytail asked.

Xander began to jog behind Melinda. He adjusted his top hat. He straightened his tuxedo as he ran. His costume was just as important as his unicorns'. He was the ringleader of this particular bizarre troupe. It was his job to set the scene and give the audience the magic they craved.

"You won't believe the size of the crowd," Melinda said as they arrived behind the large barnlike building.

For their first few shows, the Rainbow-Barfing Unicorns didn't have the luxury of a stage at all.

But when Melinda saw the audience's reaction to Xander's show, she quickly created a building to suit their purposes. She also devoted an entire small stable to the trio of unicorns as a place for them to sleep and relax.

But more often than not, they slept in the dump next door. The Rainbow-Barfing Unicorns loved to be around garbage. Melinda had no idea that trash was the only thing the unicorns could eat that didn't make them barf rainbows.

Xander walked to the side of the building and up a set of stairs. Cradie, Blep, and Ronk followed him.

"Time to give 'em what they want," Blep whispered to Cradie.

"Shh!" Cradie answered. As the unofficial leader of the group, Cradie was often shushing Blep. They wanted to thrill the audience a little bit. But they didn't want to end up on the front page of the newspaper. Barfing rainbows is one thing. Talking unicorns would have the entire world buzzing.

Luckily, Blep didn't want to end up in a science lab anymore than Cradie did. So as usual, he shushed.

"Ladies and gentleman," said Xander as he stepped into the spotlight. He removed his top hat and bowed at the huge crowd in front of them. There had to be at least a hundred people in the metal bleachers. "Allow me to introduce . . ." Xander paused for dramatic effect. Then he said in a booming voice, "The Rainbow-Barfing Unicorns!"

The crowd went wild as Cradie, Blep, and Ronk trotted onto the stage. Everyone clapped and cheered. A few people whistled.

Only one man didn't say anything. He wore an expensive tan sports coat with matching pants. This middle-aged man in his nice shoes wearing his designer watch just sat in his seat with his hands in his lap.

Then his mouth dropped open. The man in tan couldn't believe what he was seeing.

He opened his favorite blue notebook and scribbled down a single word.

"Xander."

CHAPTER THREE

"Mr. DeVon?" asked the driver in the front seat of the long black sedan. "Mr. DeVon?" she asked again.

"Hm?" Russell DeVon finally answered. He looked up from the blue notebook in his lap.

"I was saying, it was quite the show, wasn't it?" his driver said. "I promised you some local color, and I delivered, don't you think?"

"It really was—" Russell began.

"Sort of like your TV program, right?" said the driver. She was looking back and forth from the road to the rearview mirror in the center of the windshield. She seemed very interested in what her passenger had to say, even if she wasn't quite willing to let him say it.

"Oh, yeah," said Russell. "Very—"

"I just got to thinking right now," said the driver, "I'm thinking that I hope I didn't get anybody in trouble."

"In trouble?" asked Russell.

"I mean, that show is just some local boy putting on a few magic tricks for a crowd of tourists and whatnot, I'm sure he doesn't mean to be copying your show or anything."

DeVon smiled. This woman had it backward.

"It's fine," said Russell. "I'm not too worried about it."

"So you're not going to sue him?" said the driver. "Because it was a show with magic unicorns and your cartoon stars magic unicorns?"

"No," said Russell. "People know *One Trick Pony*. A grade-schooler making a little spending money isn't going to hurt us. We're a multibillion-dollar operation."

A bit relieved, the driver smiled into the rearview mirror. Then she focused once again on the winding road through the mountains in front of her. It would take less than fifteen minutes to get Mr. DeVon back to his fancy hotel. It was the most expensive hotel in town, in fact. But that only made sense. *One Trick Pony* had been one of the most popular cartoons on TV for over a decade now. And Russ DeVon was its sole creator.

"Although," said Russ, stretching out the word. "I would like to meet that young man."

"Yeah?" said the driver. "I think he goes to school somewhere around here. There was a piece about him written up in the paper not too long ago."

"Hm," said Russ. "Maybe I'll look into that."

The rest of the drive was spent in silence. The driver wasn't positive that she had gotten Xander into trouble, but she wasn't sure she hadn't either.

CHAPTER FOUR

When the bell rang, Xander nearly jumped out of his chair. He had been daydreaming again. Staring two rows in front of him in the direction of his classmate Kelly had a tendency to do that to him.

This particular daydream had been about Kelly being kidnapped by a ruthless gang of pirate space aliens. Summoning his courage and a swashbuckling ability he never knew he had,

Xander had fought off the rogue creatures. He had arrived at the point in the story where Kelly would lock eyes with him, tuck her straight brown hair behind one ear, and perhaps even grant him a kiss on the cheek.

But the incredibly obnoxious school bell had cut the adventure short. It would have to be continued until the next time he was stuck in math class, bored out of his mind.

As Xander gathered his things, he noticed Andy. Andy sat next to Xander, a situation Xander would never be comfortable with.

Andy was smiling at the moment. It wasn't a friendly grin, that much was for sure. It seemed to say, "I saw you staring at Kelly, you little weirdo."

"What?" Xander said. He lowered his rather full eyebrows.

"You're such a loser," said Andy. Then he punched Xander in the arm.

Neither the insult nor the punch particularly hurt. Either way, Xander didn't have time to think about it. Kelly was walking up to him.

"Hey," she said.

"Hey," said Xander. He tried his best to seem casual. He leaned on his desk. But then his math book slipped out from under his arm and thumped on the floor.

"Loser," Andy said again as he walked away. Fortunately for Xander, Kelly pretended not to hear the always-loud school bully.

"So," she said, "what time are you heading to Aunt Melinda's on Saturday?"

"Probably an hour or so before the show," said Xander. "Why?"

"I'm going to be there a little early," said Kelly. "Aunt Melinda wants me to show some . . . people around or something."

"Is that like a promotion from selling tickets?"

"Definitely not a promotion," said Melinda. "There's this boy she wants me to get to know. He's the son of her old high school boyfriend or something."

Xander's cheeks flushed. He didn't mean for them to. He wasn't even aware it was happening. Kelly was hanging out with some other kid? A boy? Was this like a blind date situation? He wanted to ask all of these questions. But instead he said, "Oh. Cool."

Kelly studied Xander for a moment. It was as if she was waiting for him to comment.

But all Xander said was, "Well, I have to get home. Got a lot of homework to do over the weekend, and I should get a jump on it."

With that, he rushed away, bumping into a desk as he went. It took Kelly less than thirty seconds to realize that she and Xander were in the same class. They didn't have any homework that weekend.

After he grabbed his book bag, Xander practically ran to the front of the walker's line. As soon as he was able, he shot out the door and down the steps of the school. A few seconds and a few turns later, the school was out of sight.

Xander stopped to catch his breath. "Well that was awkward," he said out loud.

"Excuse me," said a voice from the nearby street. "Xander?"

Xander looked over to see a rather fancy black sedan parked next to him. The back window was rolled down, but Xander couldn't quite see into it.

With a click, the back car door opened. A man in a fancy suit and tie stepped out. He had dark, blackish-brown hair, and eyes that seemed sunk into his face.

"Um, yeah?" Xander said.

"Hi, I'm Russell DeVon," said the man. "You might have heard about me?"

"I don't think so," said Xander. He took a step away from the car.

Xander's parents had been very clear about talking to strangers. They didn't mention it quite as much these days now that Xander was in sixth grade, but it was still a rule in his house. There was something even worse about this particular stranger. Xander didn't want to be talking with him at all. The man gave off a bad vibe.

"I'm the creator of *One Trick Pony*. The cartoon?" DeVon said. Xander stared at him blankly and took another step away. "You've had to have heard of it."

"Yeah," said Xander. "OK. Nice to meet you." Then he began to walk away.

"Xander, I want to talk with you," said DeVon. "I saw your show the other day. At the orchard."

"OK," said Xander. "Well, the show is on Saturdays and Sundays. Feel free to drop by and see it again." He did his best to sound polite and friendly, but he was certainly feeling creeped out at the moment.

"I know about the unicorns," said DeVon.

Xander froze in his tracks.

"I know they can talk," he said. "I know about Pegasia. I just don't know how you brought them back here."

Xander turned around and made eye contract with this strange man. "I have no idea what you're talking about," he said. Then he turned away again. Xander moved faster now.

"Wait," said DeVon. He took a few quick steps and grabbed Xander by the arm. Xander turned to glare at him. His eyes were wide. He was no longer creeped out. He was full on scared now. "I just want to talk," said DeVon.

"AHHH!!!" Xander yelled. The sound was so loud it caused DeVon to recoil a step. A man walking his dog across the street paused and looked over toward them.

DeVon instantly let go of Xander. "There's no need to—"

"AHHH!!!" Xander yelled.

DeVon's face went white. The man across the street moved closer. Russell looked down the block to see two older women standing in a garden. They were looking at him, too. He backed away more, and got back into his car. Within seconds, the sedan pulled away.

Xander stood in place. He didn't know what to do.

"Hey," said the man across the street with the dog. "Everything OK?"

Xander didn't answer. He just turned and ran home.

CHAPTER FIVE

Thirty-one years ago, Russ DeVon fell down a hole . . . and kept on falling. He was playing in the soybean field next to his house when it happened. His mom usually didn't let him go much farther than the backyard. But his mom wasn't watching him at that moment.

It was one of the last few days of summer there in Ohio. A cool breeze was blowing. Mrs. DeVon had been reading her book in a lawn chair, looking up at Russ from time to time. Then the phone rang inside.

She looked at Russ, and he could see her weighing the pros and cons. He was nine years old. He could be outside for a little while by himself without her supervision. And the person on the phone could be someone important. It could be Betty from the book club telling her which novel she picked for next month's meeting.

So Mrs. DeVon went inside. And less than a minute later, Russ ran into the soybean field.

He liked to pop the little beans off their stems, even though he wasn't supposed to. He also liked to lay down in the field and disappear from the world between the rows. He was doing this second thing when his mom came back out to check on him. Her phone call had ended, and she was back to obsessing over her son.

She didn't see him at first. She put her hand over her eyes to block out the afternoon sun. "Russ?" she called.

Russ didn't answer. He was sure that his mom would find him soon enough.

For now, he was enjoying being alone. If he wasn't writing in his notebook in his room, he never got to be by himself. Writing time was the only time his mom gave him any privacy. He was enjoying this extra alone time outside. Even if it would only last a minute or two more.

After calling once more, his mom walked around the side of the house to check the front yard. Russ sensed his chance. It was now or never.

Russ got up and sprinted further into the bean field. If he went fast enough, he could make it to the thin row of trees that lined the neighbor's yard. He could hide there for hours if she didn't see him. Sure, he'd be punished for it later, but it would certainly be worth it.

He had taken only three steps when the ground gave way underneath him.

Russ DeVon fell through a hole as long as a yardstick and as wide as one, too. He braced himself for impact. This ditch couldn't be that deep. But the funny thing was, Russ never hit the bottom. He just kept falling and falling.

In fact, he fell for over two hours.

When a person falls for a second, it's unnerving. When a person falls for several seconds, it becomes terrifying. Landing is the only thing on that person's mind. But when a person falls for two hours, even the experience of falling becomes almost . . . boring.

That was how Russ felt as he fell and fell. There was nothing to look at. To his right was complete darkness. It was the same to his left. He had stopped being able to see the sky above him after the first half hour. Everything was just darkness at this point. He couldn't even see his own hands any longer. He wanted nothing more but for the fall to end. But he knew that when it did end, that would be it. No one survived a fall that lasted as long as an average movie.

That is, unless some cotton candy clouds slowed the fall.

Russ tore through the first pink cloud at record speed. He hit the purple one underneath it almost as fast. He was going a little slower by the time he tore through the light blue one under that.

After a couple dozen more masses of pink floating cotton candy slowed his fall, his eyes readjusted. He was no longer plummeting down a dark hole. Now he was falling through a bright—almost sickly bright—blue-purple sky. And he didn't seem to be falling quite as fast.

Nevertheless, his panic came right back to him. He could see the ground now. He was going to crash-land in a field of green, and somehow pink, grass.

"AHHHHH!!!!" Russ screamed. It was the first noise he'd made since he started falling.

Russ punched through a few more pink clouds. At this point, he had figured out that they were in fact made of cotton candy. A bit of the strawberry flavored gunk had gotten into his mouth. It tasted delicious, but he didn't really have time to dwell on that at the moment. When he focused again on the ground, he realized he was no longer headed for the pink and green field. He was headed for something that looked like mud. It looked like an entire lake of mud.

It wouldn't break his fall, of course. Russ knew that. He would probably hit the surface of the mud just as hard as he'd hit the ground itself. After all, no one survived a fall from an airplane without a parachute.

So Russ closed his eyes. For a brief moment, he thought of his mom and how worried she would be. And then he thought of nothing at all as his body splashed into the mudlike waters of the lake.

But strangely, it didn't hurt.

Russ opened his eyes and mouth. He didn't really mean to.

His eyes didn't help him much. He could see brown. That was it. To make matters worse, the

gunk made his eyeballs sting. So he closed his
eyes again.

His mouth didn't help him, either. He certainly
couldn't breathe. Instead, he felt a thick liquid
flood onto his tongue.

It tasted liked . . . chocolate?

Russ barely had time to think the words, "That can't be right," before he passed out. The next thing he knew, he was coughing up chocolate pudding onto a field of pink grass.

"That was quite a fall you had there, little fella," he heard a voice say.

Russ opened his eyes. They still stung a bit from the chocolate. Everything looked foggy at first. He tried to speak, and found he could do that a lot easier than see.

"I'm alive?" he said through a thick cough.

"Of course you're alive!" said the voice. It was friendly, if not a bit high-pitched. It almost sounded like a cartoon character. It was not unlike the voice of a fairy or a magical imp from some animated movie. "No one dies in Pegasia!" the voice continued. The way she spoke, it almost sounded like a song.

"P-Pegasia?" said Russ. Then a scent that smelled like strawberries filled his nose. It faded away as quickly as it had arrived.

"That's right!" said the voice. "Welcome to our home!"

"Pegasia," Russ repeated before he passed out again.

CHAPTER SIX

"I'm tellin' ya'," said Blep, "I didn't eat your stinking cookies."

"Well someone here did," said Cradie. She looked more annoyed than ever. "And you know I'm going to find out who in the next few seconds."

"It was Ronk," said Blep, scratching one of the many cracks on his reddish hide.

Being a zombie unicorn meant dealing with the worst dry skin anyone could imagine. You could barely see the condition under their stage makeup. But now that the Rainbow-Barfing Unicorns were back in their stable and had washed off their various powders and blushes, it was impossible to miss their cracked and hardened skin.

"**RONK!**" Ronk said. He shook his head "no" as he brayed.

"Seriously?" said Cradie. "You're going to blame poor defenseless Ronk?"

"All I know is that it wasn't—" Blep began. But then he lunged forward. He opened his mouth. "**BLEP!**" he shouted.

At the same time, a perfect rainbow shot from his mouth. It doused the room in multi-colored light. It would have been beautiful under any other circumstance. But as it turned out, even a rainbow looks gross when it's barfed up.

After a while, the inside of the stable faded back to darkness. It was night now, and Aunt Melinda hadn't felt the need to supply the "ponies" with electricity. But the Rainbow-Barfing Unicorns didn't mind. They were up with the sun every morning, and the calm darkness of the small barn let them engage in one of their favorite zombie past times: sleep.

Xander had done his best to make the stable comfortable. The floor was covered in piles of soft straw, except for at three of the corners. Those Xander had called the "bedrooms." He had dragged three large mattresses from the dump into the stable to give the Rainbow-Barfing Unicorns all the comforts of home. And while the mattresses weren't made of marshmallows or stuffed with sugary fluff, they were soft, and the Rainbow-Barfing Unicorns had each claimed one.

There wasn't much else in the little stable. There was a feeding trough lining one wall. But that was mostly to keep up appearances.

The Rainbow-Barfing Unicorns took most of their meals at the dump. Garbage was easy on the digestion, and they didn't want to barf rainbows more than they had to. They reserved the barfing for after an occasional sweet or during the finale of their stage show. The audience loved that part. Xander called it the "show stopper."

"Aha!" said Cradie after this most recent rainbow faded away. She had a smile on her face. "I knew it! You stole my cookies!"

"That was from something else," said Blep.

"That rainbow smelled like chocolate chip," said Cradie.

"RONK," Ronk agreed.

"Fine," said Blep. "I owe ya a pack of cookies."

"Two packs," said Cradie. "I expect to be paid back for my pain and suffering."

"A pack and a half," said Blep. "And that's my final—"

There was a rustling outside the stable window. The orchard was quiet at this time of night, so it caught the Rainbow-Barfing Unicorns' attention.

"What was that?" said Blep.

Cradie perked up her ears. The rustling continued.

"Something's outside," she whispered.

Blep tensed up.

Ronk began to shake uncontrollably.

Cradie's eyes narrowed.

There was only one door to the stable. Cradie quietly made her way over to it. Blep followed. Ronk stayed put, aside from the shaking.

Cradie placed her ear against the wooden door and tried to listen through the slats. She heard the rustling again. She didn't move. She kept listening. The rustling got closer and louder.

"What is it?" Blep asked in a whisper.

"Footsteps," Cradie said.

She was sure of that now. There was a human being outside. Possibly more than one. Her theory was confirmed when she heard the metal latch on the outside of the door lift open.

The door creaked on its hinges as it was slowly pushed inward.

A figure stood in the open doorway.

The full moon in the sky lit the figure dramatically. He stepped inside the shadowy stable. He looked from one side to the other. The stable seemed to be empty. There was no sign of the Rainbow-Barfing Unicorns.

"RONK!"

Suddenly the man was knocked to the side. Two hooved feet had shot out of the shadows. The man landed face first in the straw. When he looked up, he saw another hoof smacking him directly in the forehead.

"Ah!" Russell DeVon exclaimed. His eyes darted around the inside of the stable.

Cradie, Blep, and Ronk all stepped out into the moonlight.

"**RONK!**" Ronk said again.

"I know you can talk," said Russell. "You're not fooling anyone."

Cradie didn't answer. She didn't know this trespasser. She wasn't about to reveal her deepest secrets to him.

"You're from Pegasia," said DeVon. "I know because I've been there. Years ago. Probably before you were born, even."

Cradie still didn't respond.

"Fine," said DeVon. "Have it your way." Then he got to his feet and turned his head toward the open door of the stable. "Gentlemen!" he shouted.

Blep stepped in front of Cradie and Ronk

when he saw the five men rush into the stable. He raised his hooves to strike.

And then he felt the net thrown over his head.

CHAPTER SEVEN

"Cradie!" Xander said as he flung the stable door all the way open.

Xander had noticed the door was ajar from across the lawn. He had jogged over, nearly slipping on the early morning dew in the process. He normally didn't arrive at the orchard much before his show was to start. But the combination of his creepy encounter with Russell DeVon and the fact that Kelly was showing another boy around the property today had inspired him to get his act together early this morning.

Xander had gotten up at 6:30, just as if it had been a school day. That had to be some kind of record for Xander for a weekend. But as soon as he saw that open stable door, he knew his instincts had been correct.

"Blep!" Xander yelled when Cradie didn't answer. Followed by, "Ronk!"

The stable was empty. The morning sun lit the room through the slats in the wall and the open door as brightly as if it had those electric lights Xander had asked for. Three mattresses and some straw were all that greeted the concerned sixth grader at the moment.

Xander's rational mind kicked in. He rarely used that part of his brain. Usually, he preferred to live in a world fueled by his imagination.

But the Rainbow-Barfing Unicorns were almost always in their stable at this time of day. This was a serious situation. If they weren't there, his mind told him that there was only one other place they would be.

He turned and darted out of the stable. After nearly slipping two more times on the slick grass, he passed the apple donut stand, which wasn't even cooking up its first batch of donuts yet.

Xander made his way to the back entrance of the Henderson Landfill. He pulled the gate open.

"Cradie!" he yelled again. No response.

Xander ran past an aisle of broken televisions, blenders, and what looked to be some kind of microwave or VCR. He saw absolutely no one.

"Blep!" he called. Then he turned a corner around the rusted metal outsides of an old car and the insides of an old washing machine.

"Ronk!" he yelled. When there was no answer, Xander stopped to catch his breath. Then he circled the entire dump.

When he returned to the spot by the washing machine's innards, he had all but given up hope. His friends were gone.

He sat down on the trunk of the broken-down automobile. He put his face in his hands, leaning his elbows on his knees.

The next thing he knew, he was flying through the air and crash-landing into a totem pole made up of old tires.

"RONK!" said a familiar voice behind him.

Xander looked over his shoulder when the shock finally wore off. The trunk of the car had

popped open. Inside the empty shell was Ronk.
The zombie unicorn looked quite relieved to see
his friend.

"Ronk!" Xander called, realizing that he
sounded as strange as this Rainbow-Barfing
Unicorn with the very limited vocabulary.

"RONK!" Ronk said again. He jumped out of the car's frame and galloped over to Xander.

Xander got to his feet just in time for Ronk to rub against his leg. Ronk looked like a cat greeting its owner.

"What happened here?" asked Xander.

"RONK," Ronk said, shaking his head "yes."

"Where are the others?" asked Xander.

"RONK," repeated Ronk in the same tone of voice.

"Did someone take them?" Xander asked. "How did you get away?"

"RONK."

"Was it Russell DeVon? That weird guy in the fancy suit?"

"RONK."

"I have no idea what you're trying to tell me," said Xander.

"RONK."

This was getting Xander absolutely nowhere. He pet Ronk's mangy mane. He instantly regretted this decision, however. Ronk could shower five times a day and would still manage to be absolutely filthy.

Xander wiped his rather sticky hand on his jeans. As he did, he noticed that there was something stuck to his palm.

Something other than a layer of dirt and what seemed to be the remnants of a chocolate chip cookie.

Xander peeled a small piece of paper off his palm with the fingers of his right hand. It was a receipt for a fast food restaurant right off the highway.

Xander knew the spot. This particular fast food joint was also next door to the fanciest hotel

in town. A hotel just fancy enough for someone like Russell DeVon.

"Good job, buddy," Xander said as he pet the unicorn again. Once again, he was filled with instant regret. He wiped his hand against his jeans. "Let's go," he said.

He and Ronk ran back through the orchard. They managed to only slip once on the dew.

CHAPTER EIGHT

"This isn't right," said the largest man in the room.

"Hank, I've known you for twenty years. This is the first time you've developed a conscience on a job," said the smallest man in the room.

"Huh?" said Hank. He pulled his T-shirt down over his gut for the third time that hour. It didn't make sense. The shirt fit him last time he wore it. The washing machine at the laundromat must be shrinking his stuff again.

"What's got you upset, buddy?" said the smallest man.

"I'm not saying I'm upset because we broke the law," said Hank. He sat down in one of the wooden chairs in the old dining room. He scooted it away from the dusty table. "I'm saying this ain't right because our boss outside—he thinks he can talk to ponies."

"Unicorns," said the middle-sized man already sitting at the table. His elbows rested on a dusty green place mat. "Boss says they're unicorns."

"Right," said Hank. "You're making my point for me."

"Hey," said the smallest man. He continued to pace the floor on the other side of the table. The boards squeaked underneath him. It was an old farmhouse. No one had kept it up in years and it showed. "As long as this guy's money is good,

I don't care if he has us running through the woods searching for fairies."

At this, the middle-sized man laughed.

"It's not funny, Jerry," said Hank.

"It's a little funny," said Jerry.

"OK," said the smallest man. "I'll go check on Ben and Jimmy outside. Make sure they haven't noticed any suspicious cars passing or nothing. Then I'll go talk to the boss. He probably doesn't need us for much longer now that he's got two of his precious 'unicorns.'"

"Unicorns," repeated Hank under his breath.

The smallest man smiled a grin that revealed a few regular teeth, one gold tooth, and one tooth that simply wasn't there. It seemed to match the style of his patchy beard and messy, short gray hair. He winked and walked out of the room.

"Hey, Nate," said one of the men on the porch.

"Anything?" asked this small man named Nate. He didn't bother to stop as he walked past the two guards and down the wooden, splintering front steps. The stairs desperately needed a fresh coat of white paint.

"Nope," said one of the guards. "No car even passed."

Nate didn't answer. He just nodded his head approvingly and kept walking across the large property. The grounds were as poorly maintained as the old farmhouse. The grass looked to not have been mowed in at least a season or two. It was nearly a foot high in most places. Like the house, it seemed to be slowly decaying in the sunlight.

The farmhouse's paint was peeling and chipped. Its roof was missing every third shingle. Its windows cracked and smudged. While it wasn't currently the season for it, Nate figured the house would make a great attraction come Halloween. That is, if somebody with a bit more creativity than DeVon rented it.

The property was probably a good eight to ten acres in size. By the time Nate had walked one of those acres, he had reached the barn. The unpainted shack of a building was in even worse shape than its house. The rooftop had caved in completely on one side.

But the sliding front door closed tightly enough. The walls were just the right amount of sturdy to hold their prisoners inside. Mr. DeVon's "unicorns" were nice and contained for the time being.

He knocked on the door with a heavy fist. "Boss?" he said. He could have called him Mr. DeVon, or even Russell. But Nate knew from experience that guys that wear suits like Mr. DeVon preferred to be called "Boss." They liked to know they were in charge every chance they could get.

There was a clicking of a lock and then the door slid open just a few inches. Nate could see Russell's eye peering out. Then DeVon grunted, and slid the door open a little more.

Nate stepped inside as Russell closed the door quickly behind him. Then he snapped a padlock in place over the door's metal latch.

Across the large, dirty room was a small pen. Its fence was built of rickety old boards. Nate figured the fenced off area was about ten feet by ten feet if he was being generous.

Inside, he could see DeVon's two captives: one slightly red and one slightly purple pony. Each had the sickliest looking skin Nate had ever seen. And each also had some sort of unicorn horn attached to its forehead.

"Um, any luck?" Nate asked.

Russell DeVon didn't answer. He simply walked back across the large room toward the pen. The two animals were lying on the floor at the far side of the pen, against the barn's wall. It was as if they were trying to stay as far away as possible from DeVon.

"This is ridiculous," DeVon said to them. "We've been at this for hours. Just talk to me."

Nate cringed. His boss was completely off his rocker. Dressing ponies up like unicorns was one thing. Trying to get them to talk was something else altogether.

"Is there something you want?" said DeVon. "Tell me what that is, and I'll get it for you. I'm a very rich man. I just want to have a simple conversation. Is that too much to ask?"

With that, the purple unicorn got to her feet. She walked over to an empty feeding trough and stuck her nose inside. It was empty, and after finding it so, she walked back to her spot on the ground and laid down.

"I think they're hungry, Boss," said Nate.

"No," said Russell. "They're—" He froze in place. He stared at Nate. Finally, he nodded. "You're right. Let's get them something to eat."

"All right," said Nate. "Anything in particular? Oats and hay and the like?"

"No," said Russell sharply. "Nothing like that. Stop by that candy store on Lexington Avenue. And bring a bucket."

Nate looked at DeVon and blinked.

Then he turned around, rolled his eyes, and set out to run his boss's errand.

CHAPTER NINE

"Um, hi," said Xander once he stepped up to the hotel's front desk. "Do you know if Russell DeVon is staying here?"

The friendly young woman behind the counter peered down at this boy in her lobby. He was holding the leash to what looked like a rather large dog. Or at least she thought it was a dog. The thing was wearing a bulky yellow poncho at the moment, so it was hard for her to tell.

"We don't allow pets inside this building, sir," she said.

"I'm sorry," said Xander. "He's . . . um . . . my uncle's. From when he was a kid, you know?"

The woman behind the counter did not know.

"My uncle used to live around here," Xander continued, "and his . . . um . . ."

"Dog?"

"Sure," said Xander. "His dog is getting older, so I thought he'd want to see him before he left town or whatever."

"Your uncle is Russell DeVon?" The woman seemed doubtful to say the least.

"Yes."

"And you want to reunite him with his childhood dog," the woman said.

"Yes."

The woman looked at Xander with a crinkled nose. "I think your dog needs a bath."

"I think you're right," said Xander. He flashed the biggest smile he could force.

The young woman sighed and then looked at her computer screen. "You're lucky I'm a sucker for pet owners," she said. "Let's see . . ." She typed something onto her computer and then said in a meandering voice, "Russell . . . DeVon . . ."

"He's not here," said a man walking behind the counter. "Saw him and his party leave a while back." The man was blond and spoke in a voice that sounded too gruff for someone with his boyish features.

"Did he say where he was going?" Xander asked.

The blond man looked down at him. "No pets in the hotel, kid."

"RONK!" brayed Ronk under his poncho.

"Did your dog say 'ronk?'" asked the woman.

"No," said Xander.

"RONK!" said Ronk.

"Yeah," said the man. "That thing said 'ronk.'"

"That was me," said Xander. "Did my uncle say where he was going?"

"RONK!"

"What is going on?" asked the woman. "Let me see your dog."

"Your uncle is Russell DeVon?" asked the man.

"Yeah, did he say where he was going?" Xander asked. He was getting worried now. His story was falling apart.

"Why is his head so pointy under that slicker?" asked the woman.

"I heard him mention some farmhouse," said the man. "On Gerber Road or something."

By this point, the woman was walking around the corner of the counter. She was intent on getting a better look at Ronk. That wasn't going to help things. Xander figured he had learned all he was going to learn here. He might as well finish his little play with a satisfying final act.

"That's Aunt Petunia's house!" he exclaimed. He took a few steps towards the door.

"Do you mind if I just lift up his—" said the woman as she bent down to look Ronk in the face.

"Thanks for your help!" Xander said. Then the woman lifted up Ronk's poncho.

"RONK!" the unicorn brayed.

A gush of bile splashed out from behind his crooked teeth and onto the woman's neatly pressed dress.

"Bye!" Xander said, pulling at Ronk.

Xander and Ronk sprinted out of the lobby.

As they fled, the young woman didn't say anything. She just remained crouched there on the shiny hotel floor. Her eyes were wide.

"You OK?" asked the man behind the counter.

If she answered, Xander didn't hear it. He and Ronk had already sprinted across the street. He helped Ronk into the small cargo trailer hooked up to the back of his bike.

Xander wasn't sure why he had made up an Aunt Petunia to the hotel clerk, but he did in fact have an aunt on the mind at the moment. There was a pay phone on the next block. He'd stop there to call Aunt Melinda. Then it was off to Gerber Road to search for a farmhouse that fit the bill.

"Hang on tight, Ronk," he said to the lump under the poncho.

The lump didn't answer.

Not at first anyway. It would wait until Xander had pedaled a block south before it brayed another approving, **"RONK!"**

CHAPTER TEN

Russell DeVon sat in the corner of the barn. The sun had set, and it was getting darker inside. Like the Rainbow-Barfing Unicorn's own stable, there was no electricity inside this particular rundown building.

As he sat on an overturned plastic bucket, Russell stared at the two unicorns caged in the wooden pen across from him. There was no denying who they were. He knew it from the second he saw their stage show at the orchard.

Russell wasn't sure how or why they barf rainbows now, but he recognized a real unicorn when he saw one. Even a unicorn in severe disrepair as these two odd animals seemed to be. Unlike most everyone else in the world, Russell DeVon had seen plenty of unicorns in his life.

"Thirty-one years ago, I went to Pegasia," he said.

The unicorns in the corner seemed to ignore him.

"That's how I know what you are."

There was still no response.

"I fell through a hole in the field behind my house in Ohio. When I woke up, I had splashed down in a lake made completely of chocolate pudding."

Cradie looked over at Russell.

"Sounds familiar, huh," said DeVon. "I lived with your . . . kind . . . for almost a month. And then something happened. For whatever reason, they considered me unfit to live among them. They kicked me out. Made me enter some portal, and boom, I was back in my parents' backyard."

"Do you have any idea what it's like to be thrown out of such a magical world?" Russell continued.

Cradie's face stiffened. Yet she said nothing.

"Maybe you do," said Russell. "If that's the case, you know I'd do anything to get back there. I've been daydreaming about that place my entire adult life. It's how I made my fortune. I just wrote down what I saw there, and it became one of the biggest cartoons in history."

Cradie rested her head on the barn floor.

"I want to go back," DeVon said. "I'll let you free if you just tell me how to get back."

Cradie closed her eyes.

Russell DeVon sighed, and stood up. He walked toward the sliding door exit. He pulled the key to its padlock from his pants pocket.

"What did you do?" Cradie asked quietly.

"What?" said Russell. He turned around quickly. His voice grew more excited as he said, "You can talk! I knew it!"

Cradie spoke again. She didn't bother to open her eyes. "What did you do that made them kick you out of Pegasia?"

"Nothing!" DeVon said. "I didn't do anything wrong. The high council just decided—"

"I don't know how to get back," said Cradie. She opened her eyes and got to her feet. "But I wouldn't tell you if I did."

"What?" said DeVon.

"I know who you are, Russell DeVon," said Cradie. She clenched her jaw. "Even if you won't admit it, I know what you did."

Russell's face turned a pale white. He glared at Cradie. She looked right back at him. Then he turned and hurried out of the barn. He locked the door behind him.

CHAPTER ELEVEN

Russ DeVon ran through the woods as fast as his nine-year-old legs could carry him. The only problem was, he kept tripping on candy canes. Like weeds, the little sugary red and while treats had sprouted up all throughout the woods.

Russ had never been a fan of candy canes, even when they'd show up in his stocking at

Christmas. If he wanted to taste mint, he'd brush his teeth. And one of the things he hated most in life was brushing his teeth.

His shoelace snagged on another candy cane. As he fell, he twisted to land on his side. The thing he had hidden inside his jacket was unharmed. He felt it shift around uneasily inside his jacket. But otherwise, it remained quiet.

He was almost to his destination. This whole dream was almost over. He hated to leave Pegasia, but he didn't have much of a choice. Even a fourth-grader had to eat things other than chocolate, candy, and gingerbread. He'd had a stomachache for the last two weeks from the unicorns' ridiculous diet.

If the food wasn't sweet enough, the unicorn's attitudes were even worse. Everyone giggled every two seconds. Everyone was full of cheer and

goodwill at every waking moment. It was enough
for Russ to miss his mother. The fact that she
rarely smiled would be a welcome change of
pace when he got home. And home
was just a few footsteps away.

When he reached the
clearing, Russ passed
a rock formation
that appeared
to be made of
butterscotch.
There in front
of him was a
glowing mass
of light. It
hovered a foot
off the ground.
It seemed to be

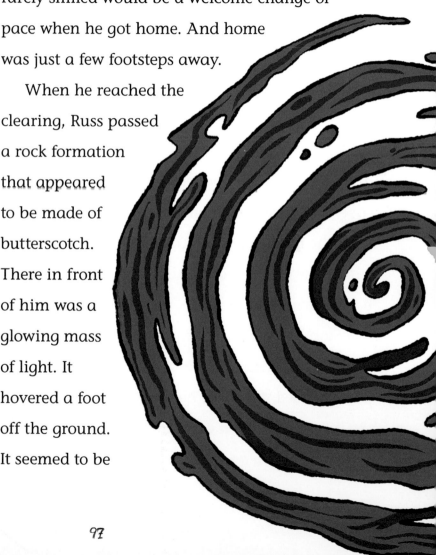

constantly swirling. It was as if it was made up of the ingredients to a new health food shake for the Pegasia citizens. A health food shake made of blueberry cream and powdered sugar.

Russ walked up to it, now at a slower pace. He felt the crunch of another candy cane beneath his shoe. When he was a foot away from the portal, he stopped. A quiet wind blew from inside the opening. It felt warm on his face.

"Stop!" shouted a stern voice from behind him. As serious as it sounded, the voice had all the intimidation of a cartoon chipmunk.

Russ turned to see a blessing of about ten unicorns. For the first time, none of them were smiling. Russ had never seen an angry unicorn during his entire month in Pegasia.

"Let her go," the unicorn in the front said. Russ recognized her. Her name was Sprinkle Shortbread. She was Pegasia's mayor.

Russ's thin jacket began to move again. Then a tiny baby unicorn popped its head out of the jacket's neck hole. Russ tried to shove the foal back inside his coat.

This little baby, the one they called Strawberry Sorbet, was to be his souvenir from Pegasia. She was going to be his pet when he brought her home to Ohio. And if he became rich and famous when people discovered his talking little friend, well then that would be a happy coincidence, wouldn't it?

Strawberry Sorbet was in no mood to be stuffed back into Russ's jacket. She saw the blessing of unicorns nearby and had decided she would rather spend time with them than this odd-smelling human being. Russ again tried to stuff her back into his jacket. He only succeeded in pricking his finger on her sharp little horn.

"Ow!" he said. He looked at his finger. And because he did, he didn't notice the sound of breaking candy canes to his right.

By the time he realized what was going on, a hoof was colliding with his stomach, and he was falling backwards through the portal. A unicorn—he wasn't sure which one—had snuck up on him and attacked. And to make matters worse, the force of the impact had knocked little baby Sorbet out of his jacket and away from the portal.

Russ DeVon was once again falling through a hole. And just as before, he was falling alone.

CHAPTER TWELVE

The small man named Nate poured a bucket full of gummy bears into the food trough in the dark barn. He was having trouble seeing. But the darkness helped in way, too.

There were so many shadows in the barn that Russell DeVon couldn't see the annoyed look on Nate's face. Nate couldn't help his expression. Who ever heard of feeding candy to ponies?

"Thank you, Nate," said DeVon. "That will be all."

"No problem, Boss," said Nate. He began to walk toward the closed and locked sliding door. Russell walked with him. He unlocked the door and then paced back toward the pen in the corner of the barn.

Inside the pen, Cradie and Blep both got to their feet. They slowly moved toward the food trough. Cradie smelled the gummy bears. She looked at Blep and nodded. The two began to eat.

"See," DeVon said. "I know your kind. I know you unicorns don't just have a sweet tooth. You have a whole set of sweet teeth."

"I'll see you later, Boss—" Nate began as he slid the barn door open. He stopped speaking when he saw a young boy standing in front of him.

Although the moon was shining, the boy was draped in shadows. The sight was unnerving and unexpected, even to a tough guy like Nate. So much so that Nate took a step backward.

And then he felt a hoof kick him right in the shins.

"RONK!"

"Yelp!" Nate exclaimed.

At that moment, Blep turned to face DeVon.
He opened his mouth wide.

"BLEP!" he brayed.

A brilliant rainbow shot from his mouth and
right into DeVon's eyes.

Blep kicked at the rickety wooden fence of
the pen. The wood snapped. Without a second's
pause, both Blep and Cradie galloped out of
the pen.

Russell shook his head. He tried to chase
after the unicorns, but his vision was still blotchy.

Nevertheless, he managed to leap in their direction.

The effort was worth it. He tackled Cradie.

Holding the unicorn around her neck, DeVon said, "You can't do this! You have to help me get back there!"

"I know what you did!" she shouted. "Strawberry Sorbet was my mother!"

Russell loosened his hold. He seemed shocked that Cradie knew the real story.

"CRADIE!" she belched as she barfed a bright rainbow in DeVon's eyes.

"Agh!" Russell said. He let go. Cradie knocked him backwards with a kick of her hind legs. Then she followed Blep out the door.

Xander, Cradie, Ronk, and Blep ran through the dark field between the old farmhouse and its barn. They headed toward the dark road beyond.

"Your bike will be too slow!" huffed Cradie.

"That's why I called them," said Xander.

Xander pointed to Gerber Road. The road was getting closer with each step. In the distance, two headlights were coming up the hill.

CHAPTER THIRTEEN

"I barely got to eat any of those gummy bears," Blep said.

Cradie did her best to ignore him. He had been making this same complaint ever since they got back to their stable at the Montgomery Orchard.

"RONK!" Ronk said. Ronk's complaint was more valid. After all, he hadn't gotten a single piece of candy.

Xander pet Ronk's mane, once again regretted it, and wiped his hand on his pant leg. He had gotten to the orchard early this morning. That made two weekend days in a row. There was no real reason this time. The Rainbow-Barfing Unicorns were safe now that Aunt Melinda had made sure DeVon had been arrested last night.

Today, Xander just felt like being with his friends.

"Hey," said a familiar voice from the doorway.

Xander turned to see Kelly framed perfectly in the morning light. He stood up and walked away from the unicorns.

"I heard about all the craziness last night," she said.

"Yeah," agreed Xander. He shoved his hands awkwardly into his pockets.

"Good thing you called Aunt Melinda and

she could pick you guys up," said Kelly. "Before that weirdo cartoon guy could try to kidnap your ponies again."

"I owe her big time," said Xander.

"She says you're even," said Kelly. "But if you feel like it, maybe you could have us over. You know, for dinner tonight? I don't know."

Suddenly, Kelly seemed as awkward as Xander. She looked away from him and tucked her hair behind one ear.

"Oh . . . uh," said Xander. "Sure. I'll ask Mom and Dad, but I don't think it'll be a problem."

Kelly smiled. Her cheeks seemed a little redder than usual.

"So you don't have to show that . . . other boy around?" Xander asked

"I only have him for the rest of the morning," said Kelly.

"Have him—?" Xander began. He was confused.

"Miss Kelly!" said a tiny voice from behind them. "I want to see the bees again!"

Kelly didn't turn around. She rolled her eyes. "I swear, this kid is obsessed with Aunt Melinda's beehives."

Xander peered down at the little five-year-old running over to them. Then he looked back at Kelly. "That's the son of Aunt Melinda's high school boyfriend?"

"Annoying, isn't he?" Kelly said in a whisper.

By that time, the little boy had grabbed Kelly's hand and was tugging on it. So Xander didn't answer.

"Bees!" the boy shouted.

"Bees it is," Kelly said. Then she smiled at Xander, "I gotta go. Let me know about tonight."

Xander waved and then walked back inside the stable.

"Woooooooo," Blep said. He sounded like a studio audience from an old TV show. Xander wondered for a moment how Blep even knew what a TV was. "Got a big date?" Blep teased.

Xander smiled and sat down on the mattress beside Cradie. She appeared lost in thought at the moment.

"You OK?" Xander asked.

"Just thinking," Cradie said.

"**RONK!**" Ronk brayed at Blep.

"No, I don't have any gummy bears," said Blep. "You think if I had gummy bears I wouldn't be eating them right this second?"

"**RONK!**" Ronk insisted.

Cradie looked down at Xander. Now they were both smiling.

Xander hugged Cradie and pet her mane. Unlike Ronk, her hair wasn't that greasy. He barely felt the need to wipe his hand on his jeans at all. He did end up wiping his hand, but it was a close call this time.

If nothing else, Xander considered that progress.

CHARACTER SPOTLIGHT:
BLEP!

Height: 5 feet, 4 inches

Horn Length: 2 inches (formerly 7)

Weight (before barfing): 165 pounds

Weight (after barfing): 145 pounds

Color: Reddish

Barf Color: Full Spectrum

Shaggy, reddish, and sporting a broken horn, Blep is the crudest of the group. He is also as sloppy as he is rude. However, Blep does harbor a soft spot when it comes to Cradie, a crush he'll deny to his dying day.

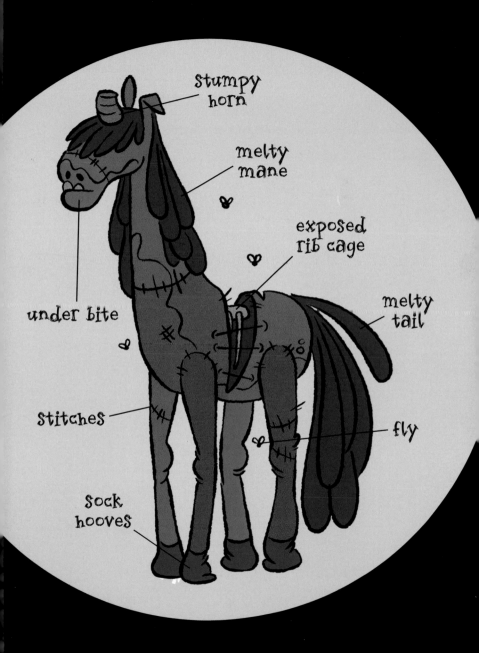

GLOSSARY

banish (BAN-ish)—to send someone away from a place and order them not to return

bray (BRAY)— to make a sound like the call of a donkey

digestion (duh-JESS-chuhn)—breaking down food in the stomach and other organs

dimension (duh-MEN-shuhn)—a place in space and time

dramatic (druh-MAT-ik)—very noticeable

expression (ek-SPRESH-uhn)—the look on someone's face

portal (POR-tuhl)—a door or passage to another place

spectrum (SPEK-truhm)—the range of colors shown when light shines through water or a prism

BARF WORDS

blow chunks (BLOW CHUHNGKS)—to barf

heave (HEEV)—to barf

hork (HORK)—to barf

hurl (HURL)—to barf

puke (PEWK)—to barf

ralph (RALF)—to barf

regurgitate (ree-GUR-juh-tate)—to barf

retch (RECH)—to barf

spew (SPYU)—to barf

throw up (THROH UHP)—to barf

upchuck (UHP-chuhk)—to barf

vomit (VOM-it)—to barf

yak (YAK)—to barf

JOKES!!

What do you call a
Rainbow-Barfing Unicorn's dad?

Pop-corn!

What kind of bow is
easiest for a Rainbow-
Barfing unicorn to tie?

A rain-bow!

What do you call
a smart Rainbow-
Barfing Unicorn?

An A-corn.

What does a Rainbow-Barfing Unicorn eat for breakfast?

Lucky Charms.

What did the Rainbow-Barfing Unicorn say when it had a sore throat from puking all day?

I'm a little hoarse!

What type of Rainbow-Barfing unicorn can jump higher than a house?

All of them. Houses can't jump!

MORE JOKES!!

What do Rainbow-Barfing
Unicorns wear to work?

UNI-forms!

What is a Rainbow-Barfing
Unicorn's favorite kind of
garbage scraps?

Unicorn on the cob.

What's a Rainbow-
Barfing Unicorn's favorite
mode of travel?

Unicycle!

Why don't Rainbow-Barfing Unicorns wear shoes?

They can't tie rain-bows!

How do Rainbow-Barfing Unicorns wash their hair?

In a bubble barf.

Why do Rainbow-Barfing unicorns always stick together?

They are a uni-fied group.

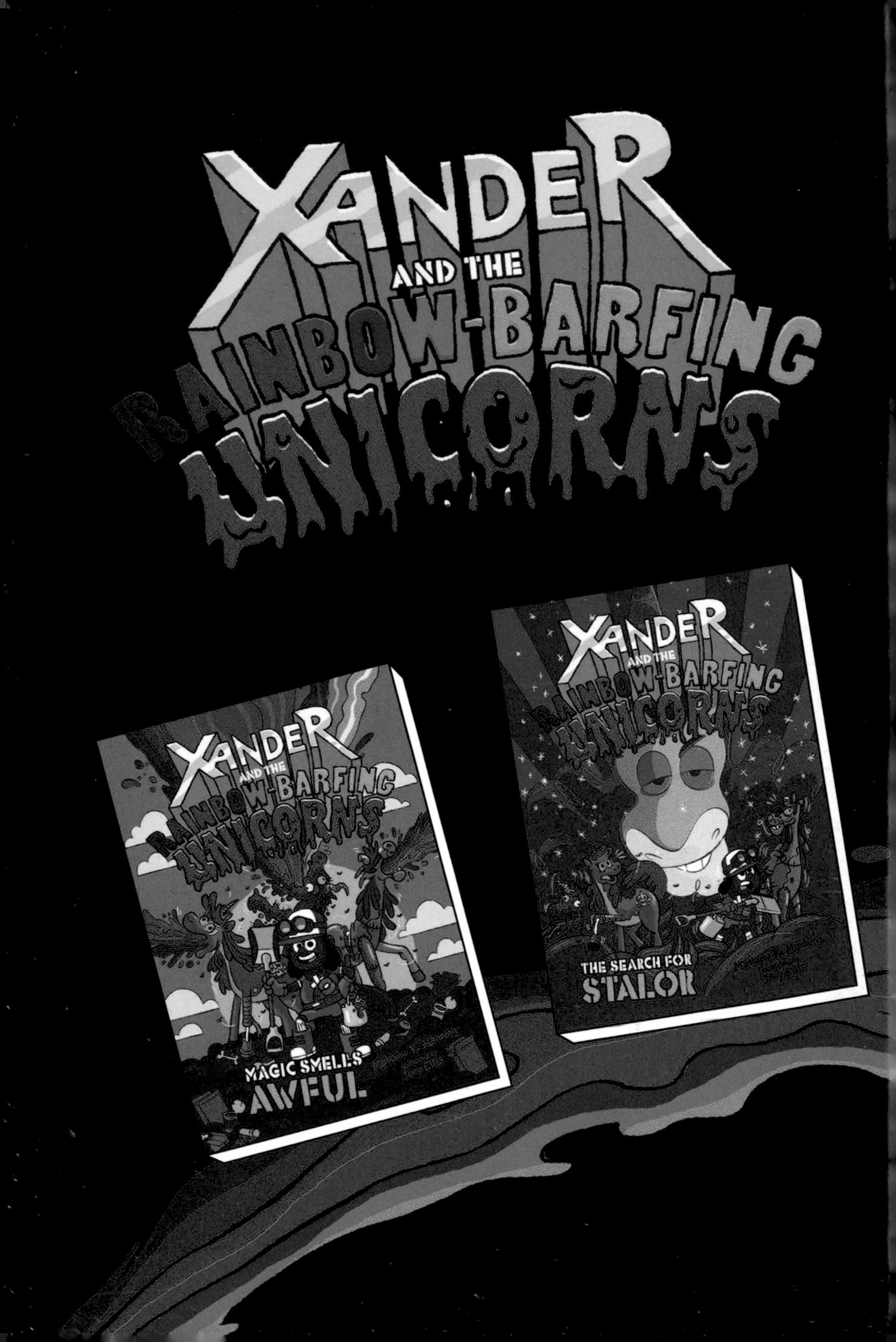
XANDER
AND THE
RAINBOW-BARFING
UNICORNS
XANDER AND THE RAINBOW-BARFING UNICORNS
MAGIC SMELLS AWFUL
XANDER AND THE RAINBOW-BARFING UNICORNS
THE SEARCH FOR STALOR

READ THEM ALL!

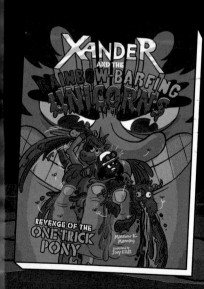

only from capstone

www.mycapstone.com

AUTHOR

The author of over seventy-five books, Matthew K. Manning has written dozens of comic books as well, including the hit *Batman/ Teenage Mutant Ninja Turtles Adventures* miniseries. Currently the writer of the new IDW comic book series *Rise of the Teenage Mutant Ninja Turtles*, Manning has also written comics starring Batman, Wonder Woman, Spider-Man, the Justice League, the Looney Tunes, and Scooby-Doo. He currently resides in Asheville, North Carolina with his wife, Dorothy, and their two daughters, Lillian and Gwendolyn.

ILLUSTRATOR

Joey Ellis lives and works in Charlotte, North Carolina, with his wife, Erin, and two sons. Joey writes and draws for books, magazines, comics, games, big companies, small companies, and everything else in between.